Junkyard Dan

Start of a New Dan

NOX PRESS

books for that extra kick to give you more power

www.NoxPress.com

Also by Elise Leonard:

The **JUNKYARD DAN** series:
Published by Nox Press

- Start of a New Dan
- Dried Blood
- Stolen?
- Gun in the Back
- Plans
- Money for Nothing
- Stuffed Animal
- Poison, Anyone?
- A Picture Tells a Thousand Dollars
- Wrapped Up

The **JUNKYARD DAN** workbooks:
AKA: Hanging Out With Junkyard Dan
Published by Nox Press

Each workbook covers two Junkyard Dan books.

The **AL'S WORLD** series:
Published by Simon & Schuster

- Book 1: Monday Morning Blitz
- Book 2: Killer Lunch Lady
- Book 3: Scared Stiff
- Book 4: Monday Morning Blitz

Junkyard Dan

Start of a New Dan

Elise Leonard

NOX PRESS

books for that extra kick to give you more power

www.NoxPress.com

Leonard, Elise
Junkyard Dan series / Start of a New Dan
ISBN: 978-0-9815694-0-6

Printed in the U.S.A.
First Nox Press printing: February 2008
Second Nox Press printing: November 2008

NOX PRESS

books for that extra kick to give you more power

For my readers, my family, my friends.

Read on,

rock on,

never give up,

live well,

and do good things!

~Elise

Chapter 1

I'd been driving all night. And most of the day.

I had no idea where I was.

Not many signs around here.

Not much of *anything*, really.

It was the perfect place. Not many people. Lots of nature.

Nature couldn't hurt you like people could.

Well, maybe.

I thought about hurricanes and wildfires. Tornadoes and nor'easters.

I guess Mother Nature *could* pack a punch.

But maybe that's because she's a woman. And maybe that's her way of telling us that *we're* hurting *her*.

But I didn't hurt Patti. I *never* hurt Patti.

No. I treated that woman with respect.

And love.

I gave her everything she asked for. Flowers. Jewelry. Clothes. Nice cars. The big house. *Everything*!

I even gave her what she *didn't* ask for.

My heart. My devotion. My loyalty.

But that wasn't enough.

Not for Patti.

It wasn't enough that I'd worked like a dog. Twelve-hour days. Day in and day out.

My job was tough.

Wall Street was a dog-eat-dog place.

I'd learned that pretty quickly.

I may not have started *out* so tough. But I became tough. At least after a few years.

All the backstabbing.

All the fake smiles.

All the hand shakes with people who were not very nice.

I did it all.

Day in and day out.

Year after year.

I became the man she wanted. So she could have all her nice things.

As long as I had Patti? It didn't matter to me what I did as a job. Because at night? I'd come home to her.

Every night.

Nights were the only thing that kept me going.

Nights with Patti.

I'd try to forget the deals and schemes of the day. The fast-paced financial trades.

The forced smiles. The lies.

At night? When I'd remove my suit jacket? I pictured myself taking off my day. My job.

Removing that world. Peeling it off and hanging it up.

Discarding it.

So I could be me. Dan Corbett. Patti's husband.

That was most important to me.

She was most important to me.

Patti.

I did what she wanted. Always.

I was the man she wanted me to be.

Someone she could brag about. Someone she was proud of.

The man she wanted.

I *became* the man she wanted. Just for her.

I was a cut-throat stock broker. I was fierce.

I was without weakness.

In the world of finance? I showed no mercy.

I was a man of power. A man people listened to.

A man whose every word was heard. Minded. And then people did what I said.

I was applauded. Looked up to.

I'm embarrassed to say, I was idolized.

All because I was trying to be the man Patti wanted.

Forcing myself to be the man Patti wanted.

But then I got a rude wake-up call.

I was *not* what Patti wanted.

Chapter 2

What Patti wanted was a 23-year-old roofer.

But not *any* 23-year-old roofer.

The 23-year-old roofer I'd hired to fix our leaky roof. The leaky roof on our big house. Our house in the suburbs.

The house that Patti had wanted.

The house I'd bought for Patti.

The house that Patti loved.

The place I'd called "home."

How did I *know* that Patti no longer wanted me?

How did I *know* what Patti now wanted?

Easy.

I knew that because she left me a note.

That's right. A note.

It said:

> Dan,
> I'm leaving you.
> I'm leaving with Neil.
> Love, Patti

The "i" in Patti was dotted with that cute little heart she always added.

But then, so was the "i" in Neil.

All of a sudden, that little heart was annoying.

Anyhow, her clothes were gone.

So was just about everything else in the house.

If it wasn't bolted down? Or built in? It was gone.

She *did* leave me my clothes though.

That was nice.

I had no idea who "Neil" was.

But then I caught on. Pretty quickly.

It was the name on the bill lying beneath Patti's note.

It said: "Roofing by Neil."

Can you believe it?

The guy comes in here! Steals my wife! Takes everything that isn't bolted down! And then leaves me a *bill*?!

He didn't even finish the roof!

In fact, he left it worse off than it started!

Of course I threw that bill in the trash!

Yeah. Like I was really going to pay *him* a dime!

But at least the bill had cleared up my question. You know. As to whom "Neil" was.

His little logo said it all.

I saw the irony. It was hard not to!

His logo said, "Roofing by Neil. He'll strip it, lay it, and nail it down for you!"

Looks like he did that, all right.

It wasn't false advertising. That's for sure.

Only I *had* thought he was referring to my *roof*.

Anyhow, so I had to hire *another* roofer.

I made sure this one was old and ugly.

He was.

He had a face like leather. Brown teeth. Many

missing.

He chewed tobacco, and spit constantly.

His aim was off.

His boots were covered with brown blotches.

Yeah. He was my guy.

He was my new roofer. (Just in case Patti came back.)

But she didn't.

Not the next day. Or the next. Or the next.

The roof got finished. And life went on.

I went to work every day.

I didn't replace the furniture.

I just waited.

Waited for Patti to return.

But she didn't.

So now my days were like torture. And so were my nights.

I had nothing left.

Only the clothes in my closet.

Patti had taken all the dressers. They'd dumped my clothes on the center of the floor.

I guess I should thank them for that.

But I didn't.

Instead, I'd folded my clothes. Then I stacked them on the floor of the closet.

I went out and bought an air mattress.

You know the type. The ones used for camping?

I bought a twin size.

I should've gone for the queen size. At least my feet wouldn't hang off the end. Nor would I fall off the thing every time I turned over.

But even *that* didn't bother me.

I wasn't sleeping much anyhow.

I was too busy picturing Patti and Neil. In my comfy bed. With my nice furniture.

Like I said. I wasn't sleeping much.

Chapter 3

Sure I was angry.

Who wouldn't be?

But I didn't think of hurting Patti. Or Neil.

Sure I missed my wife.

I loved her with everything I had. *More* than everything I had.

But... well, so it goes, I guess.

The waiting was the worst.

Waiting for her to return.

After a while, when she didn't, I knew.

I knew in my heart she wasn't coming back.

It struck like lightening. And was as painful, I'm sure.

That's when I got in the car. The moment I

realized she was never coming back.

I just needed to get away from there.

I didn't care where I was going.

It just had to be away from *there*.

I could go. I had no ties. We'd never had children.

I'd brought it up a few times.

But Patti always shot down the idea.

She said she didn't want to ruin her body.

Of course you know what *I'd* said. Stuff like, "That couldn't happen, Patti!" And "You're beautiful no matter what."

But she didn't agree.

She just kept saying she never wanted to be pregnant. Didn't want to ruin her figure.

Things like that.

I probably should have seen something from that response.

Like maybe that she was a little self-involved. Possibly selfish.

But no. I loved her. *And* was in love with her. So I saw nothing but goodness in her.

Looking back, I should have seen it.

Should have seen the writing on the wall.

But you know what they say. Hindsight is 20/20.

I *do* miss her. And I *was* angry with her.

Mostly because I felt like a fool.

But I'm not angry anymore.

I'm just… tired.

Time will heal this wound. I know that.

Time heals most things.

But it was easier to heal away from my empty house.

So I headed out.

Just me and my car.

I should be thankful.

Patti and Neil left me that.

But only because it was with me at work. While they stripped my house.

Even so, it was still mine.

So I got in my car to go for a drive.

I drove through the suburbs.

Then through the city.

Then through a different suburb.

Houses started to be further apart.

I kept driving. Heading south.

I was past the suburbs.

Cruising down the highway as if someone were after me.

But no one was.

Which made me go faster.

I'd spent all night driving. Watched the sun come up.

And kept on driving away from home.

My home.

My house.

The house that Dan and Patti shared.

The empty house with the brand new roof.

My eyes started to hurt. It was so bright out. I reached for my shades, and put them on.

"That feels better," I said to myself.

The sun had crossed the sky. It must be afternoon now.

Hm. When did *that* happen?

I think I drove for a day. Twenty-four hours.

Maybe less.

It didn't matter.

I didn't care.

I'd only care if I ran out of road.

But that didn't seem to be happening. And I doubt it would any time soon.

If I'd hit the edge of America? I'd just turn and head west.

There was lots of great land in the west.

Tons of places I'd never seen. And they were all beautiful.

I wasn't certain. But any place had to be better than home.

I checked my gas gauge.

It was on empty.

Chapter 4

I headed off the highway to find some gas.

I looked around. It sure was green here.

Not like New York City.

And not like the green of the suburbs.

That green was false. Arranged. Landscaped. Neatly ordered.

No. I was in the country now. This was different.

Natural.

Tall trees and green grass everywhere.

It was as different from my life as it could possibly be.

It was new for me. But I liked it.

It seemed peaceful.

Quiet.

Like life here would be simple. Without problems.

A part of me longed for that.

A large part of me.

Okay, to be honest? *All* of me longed for that.

A simple, quiet life? A peaceful life? Without stress? Without pain?

Was it possible?

I looked around.

I pulled my car off the road.

I stopped my car and opened my window.

The air smelled different here.

Better.

Cleaner.

I took deep breaths. My chest rose and fell with each breath.

I felt some strength come back into me.

It felt great!

I hadn't realized how shallow I'd been breathing.

How shallow I'd been breathing since Patti left.

It felt good to breathe fully.

Felt good to get clean air into my lungs.

Once again I wondered. Could life be simple? Peaceful?

Was it possible?

Just then, a bird chirped loudly.

Like he was telling me. "Yes, Dan! *Yes*, it's possible!"

I squinted and tried to find the bird.

But the trees were full.

He was well hidden.

"Good for you!" I called to the bird.

My voice rang out in the stillness.

It was so quiet there.

I must have startled the birds. Because three birds squawked and flew from the tree.

I watched and wondered.

Wondered which one had spoken to me.

They all looked alike. Just birds.

I wondered if birds looked at people and thought the same thing. To them we must all look alike. Just people.

Then my mind wandered to Patti.

Thoughts of Patti.

I wondered what it was about her that made me love her so.

I wondered why I missed her so.

I wondered why I couldn't seem to let her go. Even though it would be easier on me to do so.

I put my car in gear and eased back onto the country road.

My gas light was blinking now. I had to find gas.

Up ahead was a gas station.

I pulled in and got out of my car. Parking the car next to the pump.

There was no one else there. Plus, it didn't seem like there'd be a mad rush of customers. So I left the car there. Next to the pump.

In New York, you couldn't do that.

There were too many people.

Always someone coming up right behind you.

So you couldn't leave your car by the pump. It was rude.

Plus, you'd probably get shot.

The thought made me smile.

I don't know why. But it did.

Maybe because that would be the perfect way to end my pain.

Shot to death. At a gas station for not moving my car.

But there was no chance of that happening here.

Not out here in the boonies. Wherever "here" was.

I had no clue.

Chapter 5

All I knew was that I was west of nowhere.

Maybe south of nowhere.

But what I liked most? Was that I was in the middle of... nowhere!

I expected someone to come out.

No one did.

I waited a few minutes.

While waiting, my mind wandered.

I pictured a friendly guy. In overalls. Grease on his face and hands.

A red rag slung over his shoulder.

I pictured him walking to me. Smiling. Asking if I needed anything.

His voice was friendly. Warm. Nice.

But that was only what I'd pictured.

In reality? No one came out.

The place looked deserted.

I didn't want to just start pumping. It seemed... rude.

This gas station was old. They didn't even have the pre-pay touch pad on the pump.

You know the one. Where you swipe your credit card? So you didn't have to walk into the garage?

No. This station didn't have "pay at the pump."

At this station, you had to walk all the way into the garage.

Which, if you think about it, really wasn't very far.

Maybe fifty feet or so.

But in today's world? That seemed like a huge bother.

Like walking fifty feet was the hugest waste of time.

Like seeing a *person* was distasteful.

I thought about that.

Were we *so* busy that walking fifty feet was a terrible chore?

Was our time *so* important that we couldn't wait for a person to take our money?

I guess so.

I pictured all the gas stations at home. They *all* had "pay at the pump." Every one.

I tried to think of a gas station that didn't.

I couldn't think of one.

They all had it. For our convenience.

Because we were so busy. And important.

So totally busy and important.

I thought how silly that was.

The whole thing seemed ridiculous all of a sudden.

I smiled as I walked to the gas station.

My mind flew out of control.

I thought about how we now have personal trainers.

We *pay* people to help us work out. But we can't walk fifty feet to pay for our gas.

Maybe if we'd left things the way they were? Where you had to walk a few feet to pay your gas? We wouldn't need costly gyms or personal trainers.

All of a sudden? Life seemed so absurd to me.

My life seemed absurd to me.

I opened the door to the garage. It tinkled.

A bell was attached at the top.

That made me smile, too.

No high-tech security system. No complex, thousand-dollar set up.

No cameras with backup tapes.

Just a simple bell.

I liked that.

I was expecting to see the man in the overalls come out. The one I'd pictured a few moments before.

"I'm coming!" someone called to me.

I peeked in at the part of the garage that fixed the cars.

There were two bays.

Both bays were filled.

One had an old Mustang. From the 60s. Cherry red. Perfect condition. Its chrome was shiny and without pits.

Someone loved that car.

It was polished and gleaming.

Perfect.

A classic!

I wondered if it was restored.

It couldn't possibly be in its original condition.

I was busy staring at the car. That's why I didn't notice the guy walk over to me.

"She's sweet, huh?" the guy said.

"Beautiful," I said back.

Then I turned to look at the guy who was talking to me.

For a split second I was shocked.

Chapter 6

The guy was dressed in black.

Head to toe.

Black spiked hair. Black spiked neck collar.

Black t-shirt.

Black leather bracelets. With sharp, silver spikes.

Black pants.

Black wallet, hanging from a long silver chain.

Black combat boots.

He was a little scary.

He had huge holes in his ears. Like earrings. But huge holes.

The holes were made with these black cylinders.

He even had a black ring pierced in his cheek.

It looked like it hurt.

It wasn't infected or anything. It just didn't look comfortable.

I wanted to ask him if it hurt. But I didn't.

"So how much did you get?" the guy asked me.

"What?" I asked.

"Gas," he said. "How much?"

"Oh. I didn't pump it yet," I said.

"Why not? Your arm broken?" he asked.

His face showed that he was annoyed.

"No," I said. "I didn't know if you had to do it."

He raised his eyebrows.

He looked at me closely.

He made a decision about me. I could tell.

He scoffed a laugh. "What?! You don't know how to pump gas?"

He laughed again. Not *with* me. *At* me.

He was thinking that I was a city guy. A stupid city guy. One who didn't even know how to pump gas.

He had no respect for me. I could tell.

He looked down at me.

He actually looked down at me!

That was so different than what I was used to.

His idea of me shouldn't matter. But it did.

All of a sudden, it did.

Which was weird.

Because normally? I wouldn't care what he thought of me.

Guys like him weren't *in* my world.

"I know how to pump gas," I told the guy loudly.

Then I turned, stomped out to the pump, and filled up my car.

I could feel the guy's eyes on me. He was watching me.

His gaze seemed to burn a hole in my back.

When the tank was full, I walked back to him.

"How many gallons?" he asked.

I told him.

He nodded.

He walked to the counter. Poked the register a

few times. "That'll be thirty-six dollars and fifty-two cents."

I took out my wallet.

I didn't know how long I'd be gone. But I wanted to keep as much cash as I could. In case I needed it.

"You take credit cards?" I asked.

"Yeah."

I flipped through my credit cards. "VISA? MasterCard? Discover?" I asked.

"Yeah. All of them."

I handed him my VISA card.

He took the card and did his thing.

Just then, my stomach growled.

Really loudly.

I hoped the guy didn't hear. But he did.

He laughed. "Been on the road long?"

"Yes," I admitted.

"Need some food?" he asked.

I looked at his vending machines.

There were sandwiches in it.

I walked toward the machine.

"I wouldn't eat that if I were you," he said.

I stopped and turned. "Why not?"

"Those sandwiches have been in there since 2003. The day we got the machine."

"The *same* sandwiches?" I asked.

He nodded. "The very same."

"Why aren't they rotten?" I asked. "Or moldy?"

The guy laughed. "No one can figure that out."

"Aren't you afraid someone will buy them? And eat them?" I asked.

"Nah. Everyone knows not to."

"I didn't."

He shrugged. "You're not from around here."

"So strangers can eat them and get sick? *That's* okay with you?" I asked. I was a little upset that I almost ate that sandwich!

What if he weren't there to stop me?

I'd have food poisoning by now.

I'd be getting my stomach pumped about now. Or I'd be dead.

Again, I smiled at the thought.

I thought of my obituary:

Dan Corbett. Died of an old egg salad sandwich.

Wouldn't Patti feel bad then!

"We rarely get strangers," the guy said simply.

Chapter 7

My stomach growled again. Loudly.

"You should go to the diner," the guy said.

He hitched his thumb over his shoulder.

"It's down the road a piece," he added.

I nodded. "Which diner?" I asked.

He snorted a laugh. "There's only one."

"On what street?" I asked.

He snorted again. "There's only one."

"There's only *one* street in this town?" I asked.

He looked at me like I was an idiot. "No. There's only one street for businesses. Main Street."

"Oh," I nodded.

"We've got other streets. *Houses* are on those."

He stared at me. His eyes squinting.

"You okay, dude?" he asked.

I shrugged. "I'm okay. Been better, I guess."

The guy nodded. "Go to the diner. Have some of Hilda's pie. It'll cure whatever ails you! Take my word."

Then he stuck out his hand.

"My name's Bubba. I own this place. Love cars."

I shook his hand.

"I know," he said. "I don't look like a 'Bubba.'"

I was thinking that. But I'd never say it.

I didn't think he'd be too pleased if I'd said it. (Plus, I didn't want to get my butt kicked.)

"My parents chose the name," he went on. "It's my given name. Not a nickname. Can you believe it?"

I looked at the pierced, black-clad guy.

Some would call his look "Goth."

I don't know what *I'd* call his look. But it sure wasn't what I'd pictured a "Bubba" to look like.

"No. It's hard to believe," I admitted.

We stood there a moment.

"I'm Dan," I said.

That made him laugh. "You don't look like a Dan," he said.

Hm. "I don't?"

"No. You look more like a Daniel. No. A Donald. That's it. You look like a Donald."

I knew what he meant.

I grinned crookedly. "I look stuffy, huh?"

"A little," he said.

I nodded.

We'd run out of things to say. But not my stomach. It was talking up a storm.

"Well, go on down to the diner. Say hi to Hilda for me," Bubba said with a laugh.

We shook hands again and I left.

I wondered how he knew "Hilda" would be at the diner. Did he know everyone's schedule in this town?

That struck me as odd.

But the thought left as quickly as it came.

I drove up the road. It took a while, but I finally hit the diner.

I parked right in front.

In New York, that would be a prized spot. But here? It seemed normal that one could park where they needed to park.

It was nice not having to circle around for a change.

Circling and searching for a parking spot. That's what I was used to.

I got out of the car. Locked it. Then reached in my pocket for some change. To feed the meter.

Only problem was, I had no change.

But that was okay. There were no meters.

I tried to think. Let's see. The last time I went out for lunch without paying for parking?

Hm. I couldn't recall.

That's how long ago it was.

I looked around and smiled.

Free parking. At lunchtime. It was a nice change.

I walked into the diner.

The booths were all empty.

There was one guy sitting at the counter.

I looked at the seats at the counter.

They were little round mushrooms. Topped with red vinyl.

Some were cracked.

They didn't look too comfortable. And to be honest? I wanted to sit and relax a bit. Enjoy my late lunch.

I hadn't been eating well lately. Didn't feel like eating much.

But the smells in this place were great!

The scent of rich brown gravy hung in the air.

Sweet apple pie sifted toward my nose.

My stomach growled again.

A short stout woman bustled over.

"Eww, you sound hungry!" she said before whistling.

I smiled shyly.

"I'm gonna feed you till those hunger pangs are gone, dearie," she added.

She plucked a menu off the counter.

"Follow me, honey," she said.

I followed her to a booth.

"This one okay?" she asked.

"Perfect. Thanks," I answered.

I slid into the booth. Slid right over the red plastic seat.

It was more comfortable then it looked.

I bounced around a little to get comfy.

"Ready to order?" she asked.

I looked at her apron. Her name was sewn into it. Up on the top. It said: Hilda.

"Oh," I said. "So you're Hilda. Bubba from the gas station said to say hi."

Hilda screeched with laughter. "Bubba from the gas station? That's funny!"

I didn't know what was so funny. But her laughter made me laugh.

"He's a real sweetie-pie, that Bubba!" Hilda said.

I didn't know what to say to that. So I said nothing.

I looked at the menu. It all looked good. I couldn't make up my mind.

"Want the blue plate special?" she asked.

"What's the blue plate special?"

Chapter 8

"Turkey, gravy, mashed potatoes, and green beans. Stuffing too. Oh, and cranberry sauce," Hilda said.

"Sounds perfect," I stated. And it did.

It was the perfect meal. Just what I wanted.

"Can I get apple pie for dessert?" I asked Hilda.

"Does a bat poop guano?" she replied.

I didn't know what she was talking about.

"I don't know," I responded. "Does it?"

I hadn't a clue.

"It sure does, honey!" she bellowed with a cackling laugh.

"So is that a yes?" I asked. "On the pie?"

"Sure is, dearie!" she said. "If you behave

yourself? I may even make it pie a la mode."

I got excited. It was embarrassing to admit. But I actually got excited. "With vanilla ice cream?" I asked.

She cackled again. "Sure enough, honey. I had you pegged as a vanilla man!"

"You did?" That was amazing, I thought.

She really knew her business.

"Sure did, toots. The *minute* you walked in the door. I said to myself, 'Hilda? That man's vanilla.'"

She filled a glass with water.

"Want some coffee or some pop?" she asked.

Pop? She must mean soda.

"Sure. I'll have some root beer if you have it."

I hadn't had root beer in years. But all of a sudden, I had a craving.

She nodded. Then she turned and hurried toward the kitchen.

I looked out the window.

I don't think two cars passed by while I'd been there.

And I was on Main Street.

It was weird. But great.

I liked it.

No one was around.

It was peaceful. Quiet.

The air was clean.

I could breathe here.

And the people all seemed happy.

Like they were doing exactly what they wanted to do.

I wondered what *I* wanted to do.

I knew what I did for a living. But I didn't like it. And I certainly didn't *want* to do it.

I kept staring out the window.

I don't know for how long.

But nothing changed.

I liked that.

A car would drive by, rarely. But it would mosey by. It didn't speed by.

No one was in a hurry.

No one seemed to have anywhere to rush to.

"Here you go," Hilda said. She put the plate

down in front of me.

It looked and smelled delicious.

"Wow, Hilda. This looks great! Better than Thanksgiving!"

Hilda smiled widely. "Music to my ears."

She set the root beer down too.

It was in a frosted mug.

"Perfect," I said with glee.

"Enjoy," was all she said.

She left to go back into the kitchen.

Chapter 9

The turkey was perfect. Moist. Not dry.

And the gravy? Amazing. No lumps. Just good rich flavor. And not too salty. Just right.

The stuffing was amazing. Better than they served at the Four Seasons during the holidays. And I'd always thought that couldn't be beaten.

Hilda's stuffing won *hands down*!

The green beans were just right. Not too hard. Not too soft or mushy. Perfect.

I couldn't remember eating such a perfect meal.

And I'd eaten in all the best restaurants in New York City.

But this? This was heaven.

Good ol' home cooking. I guess you couldn't

top that.

I savored each bite.

I was hungry, but I didn't want the meal to end.

"Everything okay here?" Hilda asked as she bustled over.

"It's perfect, Hilda! Just perfect."

She smiled. "Want seconds?" she asked. "It's on the house."

On the house? *Those* were words I hadn't heard in a long while. If ever!

"I'd *love* seconds!"

Hilda nodded. "I'll get you another plate. Anything you want me to leave off?"

"Nothing!" I said. "Bring me more of everything, please."

Hilda batted her eyelashes. "Since you said 'please,' I will. Glad you like it."

"Like it?!" I stammered. "I *love* it! I love it *all*!"

In a few minutes, she returned with another plate.

"Hilda? You're amazing!" I said.

And I meant it.

The second plate tasted as good as the first.

So it wasn't just that I was hungry.

This woman could *cook*!

I ate in silence. Enjoying each bite. Knowing it would be a long time before I ate like this again.

When I was done? Hilda came to remove the dish.

"Still want that dessert?" she asked.

"Sure do! I can't wait to taste your apple pie."

"Want it warm or cold?" she asked. "People like it different ways."

I thought about it. "Warm. With vanilla ice cream. That would be great," I said.

She nodded and took off with the dirty dishes.

Five minutes later she was back.

"How's this look?" she asked as she placed the pie a la mode before me.

The ice cream was melting over the warm pie.

"Amazing," I answered.

I picked up my fork and dug in.

"Oh, my God!" I murmured.

She nodded and started to walk away.

"Wait," I said.

She stopped short.

"Please join me, Hilda," I said.

Okay. So I was a little lonely.

Sure, I wanted peace and quiet. I wanted to be left alone in general. But a meal like this? It should be shared.

She nodded. "Want some coffee?" she asked.

"Sure," I said over a mouthful of pie.

I think I groaned with pleasure.

I heard Hilda laugh.

She came back to the table with two steaming cups.

She fiddled with the cream and sugar, asking how I took mine.

When she was done, she laughed.

"You're great for my ego," she said.

I stuffed more pie in my mouth.

Now I knew why they called it a pie hole.

"Bubba was right. This is the best pie I've *ever* had!"

She laughed with pleasure.

"Did you ever think of mass producing this?" I said.

"No," she said simply.

"You'd make a *fortune*!" I told her.

She nodded. "Maybe. But then the pleasure would be gone."

"What pleasure?" I asked around another forkful.

"The pleasure of watching people enjoy it."

I looked at her. She was watching me. Smiling. Enjoying *my* enjoyment.

Hm. She looked totally fulfilled.

She wasn't rich. She worked hard.

But she was fulfilled.

And happy.

I envied her.

Chapter 10

I stayed as long as I could in Hilda's diner.

I found comfort there.

And I know this will sound silly. But I felt as if I'd made a friend.

A *real* friend.

Someone I could count on.

It was rare to meet someone like that.

At least to feel that right away.

Most people were guarded.

They had layers of... I don't know... something around them. Protecting them. Keeping them safe. Secure.

Walled in.

Heck, *I* had those layers.

I had them *before* Patti left me.

After she took off? I think I added about thirty more layers.

I was too vulnerable. It was too easy to hurt me after she left. I *needed* those extra layers. Needed to shield myself.

But I didn't sense those layers around Hilda.

Nor did I sense them on Bubba.

It surprised me when I realized that.

I tried to leave a big tip for Hilda. But she refused to take it.

"Dan!" she called after me. "You left your money on the table."

She rushed up behind me. Before I was out the door.

She shoved the fifty-dollar bill I'd left for her into my hand.

"No, Hilda. That's for you," I said.

I tried to give it back.

"But you *paid* for your meal," she argued.

"That's your tip," I said.

She gasped.

Then shook her head.

"No. No. It's way too much," she said.

She shoved the large bill back at me. Refused to take it.

"I just wanted to thank you for the great meal. And the nice company," I explained.

She shook her head. "No. It's too much."

I took out my wallet. I put the fifty-dollar bill back inside.

I took out a twenty.

She shook her head again. "No."

I put it back. Then I took out a ten.

I handed it to her.

"No," she said. "It's still too much."

I chuckled at the situation.

It was the first time I'd ever been yelled at by a waitress for leaving too large a tip.

I took out a five. "Just take this, Hilda! I have to insist."

She finally took it. But she didn't look happy about it.

"If you want to do something for me?" she said

simply. "Just come back again. Okay?"

The thought of coming back made me happy.

But then I thought of how far away I lived.

I didn't even know where this town *was*!

I knew it was about twenty to twenty four hours *away*! But I had no *idea* where the town was. Or even what the town's name was.

I was overcome with sadness.

I'd found a place that was simple and quiet and good. And it was out of my reach.

"I'll try to come back," I said to Hilda.

For some strange reason, I gave her a hug.

She accepted it freely.

Even hugged me back.

It felt good.

In New York, people didn't hug. Strangers didn't hug. Not out of the blue like that.

It just wasn't done.

But here. Wherever "here" was. It seemed to be okay.

"You come back soon, Dan," Hilda said.

My heart sank all the way back to my car.

Chapter 11

I left the diner. But I didn't feel like leaving the town.

Not just yet.

I wanted a little more time here.

I needed a little more time here.

I'd only been there for a little while. But already I felt as if I were healing a bit.

Not a great deal. But a bit.

And a bit was more than I'd healed before.

The thought of going back to that house? It seemed unthinkable.

The thought of going back to my job? It seemed hopeless.

Joyless.

That was my life now.

Joyless.

Without joy.

Sad. Unhappy. Lonely. Alone.

The words tumbled though my mind as I drove around the little town.

I was reaching the far outreach of the town now.

The houses were no longer in sight.

More trees and grass and woods could be seen.

It was getting desolate.

Abandoned.

But in a good way.

A quiet way. A peaceful way.

A simple, uncomplicated way.

Things seemed easy here. No problems. Undisturbed.

That was how I wanted my life.

I slowed my car down before I was out of the town.

On my right was a tall wooden fence.

It was about seven feet tall, dark wood.

It was an old fence. But it was a sturdy fence.

And on the fence was a sign.

A white sign with big red letters. It said:

```
┌─────────────────────────┐
│                         │
│       FOR SALE          │
│       JUNKYARD          │
│                         │
└─────────────────────────┘
```

Then it listed a phone number.

I took out my cell phone and dialed the number.

I had no idea what made me do it. It was an impulse.

Of course, there was no reception there.

So I spun my car around and headed back for town.

I kept hitting redial.

Finally, about five blocks from the diner, I got a signal.

The call went through.

I was so afraid I'd lose the call, I slammed the brakes of my car.

I just stopped.

Right in the middle of the road.

I couldn't have the call dropped.

Not now.

Not now that I'd gotten through.

I pulled off the road as the call connected.

"Hello?" someone answered.

"Hi. I'm calling about the property."

"What property?" he asked.

"The junkyard," I said.

"What about it?"

"I don't know," I said. "I thought *you* could tell *me* about it."

There was a tiny pause on the other end. Like he couldn't make heads or tails of this conversation.

"It's a junkyard," he finally said.

"Yes," I said. "I sort of got that."

"Well what more do ya need to know?" he asked.

Wow, was this guy cranky!

"Are you the owner?" I asked.

"No," he said. "The owner died."

"Oh. Is his estate in probate?" I asked.

More silence.

"He *had* no estate, Mister. He was poor. He had nothing to probate. Or whatever that means."

The guy was even crankier than before.

"So who are you?" I asked.

"I'm the daggone idiot who was his best friend," he shouted.

"Oh," I said. I had no idea what else to say. "That's nice," I added.

"No it's not," he hollered. "I'm the imbecile who promised him, on his deathbed, to sell the junkyard. And like a buffoon, I promised to donate the profits to the local animal shelter."

"Oh," I said again. And again, I had no idea what to say. "That's nice," I added, again.

"So you want to buy it? Or what?" he barked.

"What kind of junkyard is it?" I asked.

"For cars," he snapped. "People come to you to buy parts. Like Bubba's garage. Bubba was Dan's best customer."

"Dan?" I asked.

"Yeah. Dan. Junkyard Dan. Everybody knew

him. Didn't you?"

Junkyard Dan?

It seemed like an omen.

Seemed like fate.

Seemed like someone was telling me something.

Like this was meant to be.

"No. I didn't know him. I'm sorry," I said.

"So do you want to buy it or not?! I'm missing my soaps!" he squawked.

Chapter 12

"How much is it?" I asked.

"Make an offer," he snarled.

Sight unseen, I made an offer.

"Sold!" the cranky guy said.

"Do you want me to draw up a contract?" I asked him.

"No. I trust you, Mister. Just drop off the money to the animal shelter."

"What about the keys? The title? The insurance? The deed?" I asked.

"The keys are next to the big rock by the front gate."

"Which rock?" I asked.

"The one with a big red X painted on it."

"What about the title?" I asked.

"Go to the courthouse tomorrow. Tell Judge Simpkins you bought the place. He'll handle all that stuff for you."

"Don't you want to go with me?"

"Nah. He'll call me. I'll tell him you bought it. He'll call the animal shelter to see if you gave them the money. And *I'll* call the animal shelter and make sure you gave them what we agreed on."

Sounded like a plan.

Not quite the way we did business in New York. But it seemed to be a plan.

"And the deed?"

"Judge Simpkins will handle it. Aren't you *listening*?!" he howled.

I hated to get him further riled up. But this was business. And things needed to be discussed. Soaps or no soaps.

But I tried to keep it brief. For his sake.

"What about the insurance?" I asked him. "I'd like to keep it insured by the same place."

"Insurance?!" The old guy cursed. "It's a

junkyard, man!"

"So?" I asked.

"So there *is* no insurance!"

"Oh," I said quietly. "Okay then."

"Are we *done* here?" the cranky guy roared.

"Yes, I guess so," I said. "If I should have any more questions, may I call you?" I asked him.

"No."

Then the phone went dead.

Okay. So much for the pleasantries.

"I think that went well," I said to myself.

I found myself smiling widely.

I didn't know what to do next.

So I drove back toward the junkyard.

My junkyard.

Then it hit me.

A *junkyard*?! What did I just *do*?!

What was I going to do with a *junkyard*?!

I wasn't one to freak out.

I didn't even really freak out when Patti left me.

But suddenly, I freaked out.

What the heck was I thinking about?!

What did I know about running a junkyard?!

What did one have to *do* to run a junkyard?!

I got to the junkyard and found the front gate.

There were two handles that were tied together with a chain. The lock joined the two ends of the chain. That was all that kept the gate doors closed.

It wasn't very high tech.

Anyone with a hammer could smash the lock. And then open the gate.

But I decided to get the key. By the big rock. With the red X painted on it.

Once I was at the gate? It was hard to miss.

In fact. If you walked to the gate? You couldn't *help* but notice the rock with the big red X.

Not the best hiding place one could find.

That's for sure.

I got the key. I unlocked the old lock.

And swung the doors wide open.

I was excited to look at my new purchase.

My new venture.

My new business.

Chapter 13

I took two steps into the place. Then it hit me.

I wasn't sure *what* hit me.

But it hit me.

All I knew was that I was flat on my back. With my breath knocked out of me.

And my face was covered with slime.

When I opened my eyes I saw it. Well, saw *them*.

There were about ten dogs around me and on me.

Some were licking my face. Others were prancing all over me.

While still others were sniffing me. Some in very private places.

"Hey, guys," I said aloud.

Big mistake.

One of the dogs French kissed me.

I jumped up with disgust.

"Whoa, guys. Calm down," I said.

Their tails were wagging and they looked happy to see me.

Well, not *me*. Just anyone.

They seemed lonely. Even though there were about a dozen of them.

I counted.

They were moving around a lot. But I counted twice.

Thirteen.

Junkyard Dan had *thirteen* dogs!

No wonder he wanted the money donated to the animal shelter. This man seemed to rescue all the dogs in the entire town!

Then I noticed the cats.

They were dotted everywhere.

On cars, on the fence, on the ground.

Black ones. White ones. Orange ones. Mixed-colored ones.

One came between the dogs and slid against my legs.

Rubbing me with her back arched.

She had no fear. The dogs were barking at her. But she didn't care.

She looked up at me and purred loudly.

That's when I noticed. She was missing an eye.

The poor thing only had one eye.

I reached down and scratched her head.

That was a big mistake.

Because the rest of the menagerie then wanted attention.

I felt sorry for them since their best friend was gone.

So I spent the next half hour or so petting, rubbing, scratching and talking to all the animals.

You know? It wasn't so bad.

It kind of felt good.

They sure did enjoy it!

And it felt good to know that I could make them so happy with just a little attention.

Patti didn't want pets.

She wanted white carpets. So she got white carpets. And that was not good for pets.

But all of a sudden, I saw what I'd missed.

One dog brought me a ball.

I threw it. Then watched as about eight of them took off to retrieve it.

I made a mental note to myself.

Buy more balls!

Since most of the gang was off vying for the one ball? I took that free time to walk to the office.

How did I know it was the office? Easy. It said OFFICE in big red letters over the door.

I closed the door so the dogs couldn't get in.

But they didn't seem to *want* to come in.

That was good.

They were outside dogs.

I couldn't picture thirteen dogs in this small room at once.

I couldn't picture two dogs in this small room at once.

Suddenly, the phone rang.

The sound pierced through the office.

And it seemed to echo outside, too.

That was weird.

It must have speakers or something.

I picked up the phone. "Hello?" I said.

"Is this Junkyard Dan?" a man asked.

"No, sorry."

"Who is this?" he asked.

"The new owner of the junkyard."

"Oh. Great. And your name is?"

"Dan," I said.

He paused. "Is this a joke?"

I laughed. "No, no joke."

"Do you mind if I call you Junkyard Dan? I'm sort of used to the name."

I thought about that. "No. Not really. Go ahead. Call me whatever you'd like."

"Great," the guy said. "Well, Junkyard Dan. I bought some car parts from your place. About a couple of months ago. To refurbish my son's car. You probably don't remember."

"No. I wasn't here at the time. Sorry. Today's,

ah, my first day. Sort of."

"Okay, well. You mind if I stop by the junkyard to talk to you? Tomorrow? In the afternoon?" he asked. "Since you're the new owner?"

Tomorrow? Well, I *did* have to go see Judge Simpkins. And I *did* have to get the money to the animal shelter. And it *was* probably too late to do that today.

"Sure. Tomorrow afternoon is great. I'll be here," I told him.

Chapter 14

After I hung up with… my customer, I felt great.

Ah. A nice, simple life.

Peaceful. Quiet.

Well, except for the dogs.

But they seemed to be calming down now.

That was good.

I didn't have cell reception. It seemed the junkyard wasn't near a tower.

But I used my cell to find an important number.

Dora. One of Patti's close friends.

She was a realtor.

A real go-getter.

Could sell anything!

I figured that since I was buying the junkyard, the phone on the desk came with it.

Hey, I'd pay the bill. So I could use it.

I called Dora.

When she heard it was me? She sounded… uneasy.

So, she'd heard about Patti and Neil.

Oh well. I needed something done. And needed it done fast.

And like ripping a Band-Aid off a wound? It was better if done quickly.

"Hi Dora," I said.

"If you want info on Patti? I can't give it to you. I promised," she said.

"No thanks," I said. "I'm calling to ask you to sell my house."

That shocked her. "*Patti's* house?"

"No," I said calmly. "*My* house. The one I bought for Patti. But she's no longer there."

That startled her.

"You want the listing? Or should I go elsewhere?" I asked.

"No. No. I want it," she said.

"The only thing is that you can't sell it to Patti. Or Neil. I'll sell to anyone else. At *any* price. Just get rid of it," I said.

"*Any* p-p-price?" she stammered.

"Dump it if you have to. I don't care. But if I find out you sold it to Patti or Neil. I'll *destroy* your business. Got it?" I asked her.

She knew I could do it.

I had that reputation.

I didn't *like* having that reputation. But I had it.

"Got it," she said. "But don't worry about having to give it away. It's a beautiful house!"

"Plus you work on commission, right?" I said knowingly.

"Right," she said nervously.

"So sell it. As soon as you can. Call my cell, and leave a message. I'll get back to you when I can," I said.

I didn't want her to know I bought a junkyard. Or that I didn't have cell reception where I was.

It was none of her business.

Plus, I didn't want it getting back to Patti.

I needed to start a new life. Without her. On my own.

A life *I* wanted.

A peaceful life.

A simple life.

No problems.

No backstabbing.

No 23-year-old roofers.

I figured Dora could leave a message. And I'd get back to her when I went into town.

"Okay, Dan. Thanks for your trust," she said.

It was her usual spiel.

I didn't trust her. Does one trust a snake? Could one? No.

But she was good at what she did.

And the sooner I sold that house? The sooner I could move on.

And I was ready to move on.

I hung up and then walked around.

It seemed that Junkyard Dan lived at the yard too.

He had a nice setup behind the office.

I checked it out.

I opened the closets. I looked in the pantry.

He was a simple man. Living a simple life.

He didn't seem to need much.

But what he had was okay.

Not the finest. But not the cheapest either.

I began to like Junkyard Dan.

He seemed to be a good man.

His animals prove he had a good heart. And compassion.

His possessions showed he had pride. And dignity.

He may have owned a junkyard. But Junkyard Dan was a good man.

I could tell.

I'd be lucky to follow in his footsteps.

He had framed pictures on the dresser. They were very old. At least forty, maybe fifty years old.

The pictures were faded and worn. Cracking in places.

They showed some young boys, and a man and woman. Probably his folks.

The adults in the picture were long gone, I'm sure.

But they all looked happy.

One couldn't ask for more than that.

I touched the pictures.

"Nothing shameful about this man," I said to myself.

Then I went to look for food for the animals.

It must be time for their dinner.

I fed them, then drove back to the diner.

I was surprised. Hilda was still there.

"Hi Hilda," I said as I walked back into the diner.

"Twice in one day!" Hilda said with a huge smile. "I'm honored!"

"Hey," I told her. "*I'm* the lucky one!"

Her laughter tinkled in the food-scented air.

"Mmmm. What's that smell?" I asked.

"Roast beef."

"Is it on the menu?" I asked.

"It's the blue plate special," she said.

That made me laugh. "I don't even want to know what's on the menu. From now on? I'm just ordering the blue plate special!"

Hilda cackled loudly.

"From now on?" she asked me.

"Yes," I said. "I just bought the junkyard. Looks like I'm the newest resident of…"

Then it hit me.

"Hey. What *is* the name of this town?!"

"You don't know?" Hilda asked.

I shook my head.

Chapter 15

"Well, welcome to Peaceville," Hilda said.

Peaceville? That *had* to be an omen. A good sign.

I was grinning ear to ear.

"What state are we in?" I asked her.

She cracked up. "You don't even know what *state* you're in?"

"Not really," I said with a grin.

"Guess," Hilda said.

"Are we in Georgia?" I asked.

"Nope," Hilda said.

"Florida?" I asked.

"Bingo," Hilda said.

I nodded. "Okay then. Peaceville, Florida," I

said. I wanted to hear how it felt saying it.

"Peaceville, Florida," Hilda repeated.

"I'm going to love it here. I can tell."

Hilda was so excited, she gave me a hug.

Just then, Bubba came in.

"Hey, Dan," he said. "What are *you* still doing here? I thought you were breezing right through town."

"He bought the junkyard," Hilda said. She was so excited she looked like she would burst.

"Not so great with the secrets, are you, Hilda?!" Bubba teased.

"Oh," she said to me. "I'm sorry. Was it a secret?"

She looked all upset.

"No," I told her. "Not at all. It's no secret."

Hilda punched Bubba on the arm. "You get me every time, wise guy!"

We all laughed.

"I'll sit in my usual booth, Madam," Bubba said to Hilda.

She led the way.

"Care to join me?" Bubba asked me.

I thought about that.

I wasn't sure if I should start up a friendship. I wanted my new life to be peaceful. And simple.

But Bubba and Hilda were good people.

"Sure. I'd love to, Bubba. Thanks," I said.

We both had the roast beef. And for dessert, I tried the cherry pie. A la mode.

The cherry was as good as the apple.

The meal was amazing!

"Is there anything Hilda can't cook?" I asked aloud.

"There's stuff she *won't* cook. But not stuff she *can't* cook," Bubba said loudly. Hilda laughed at his answer.

"What's so funny?" I asked.

"I love liver and onions!" Bubba said. "But she won't make it for me."

"That's because no one else will eat it in this town!" she replied.

"You know what everyone eats? In this entire *town*?!" I asked.

She smiled proudly. "Sure do."

"It's a small town," Bubba supplied.

"A *very* small town," Hilda said with a cackle.

"But welcome to Peaceville, Dan," Bubba said.

"Tomorrow I'll see Judge Simpkins. Then it'll be all set," I told them.

"Did you call the number on the sign?" Bubba asked.

"Yes," I said.

"And did you make a deal?" Bubba asked.

"Yes," I said.

"Then according to Peaceville ways? You *already* own it," Bubba stated.

"I know. It was weird. He didn't even want anything in *writing*!" I said.

"In this town," Hilda said. "Your word's your bond."

That was shocking. "There aren't too many places around where that's the way things go," I said.

"It is here," Bubba said. "Nice, huh?"

I nodded. "It *is*."

"Plus," Bubba added. "You can be yourself, and no one cares."

I looked at the piercing on his cheek. And his spiked black leather collar.

"That's nice," I said.

"So welcome to Peaceville, Dan. I'll be seeing you around, I'm sure. I did a lot of business with Junkyard Dan."

Then it must've hit him.

"Hey! Junkyard Dan! And *you're* Dan. That's funny!"

I rolled my eyes. "I've already told someone to call me Junkyard Dan. Don't see why you can't too, if you want to."

Bubba nodded. "Okay. Cool, Junkyard Dan."

His awe at the twist of fate made me smile.

It was a wonder to me too. Such a coincidence!

"He seemed like a good man," I said solemnly.

"He was a good man," Hilda said.

"He'll be sorely missed," Bubba added.

"But… now we have you," Hilda said with a chuckle.

Chapter 16

That night I played with the dogs.

Then I went to bed.

Junkyard Dan's bed was comfortable.

He must've been a big man. He had a big bed.

But it didn't feel like the bed Patti and I shared.

This felt new.

I slept soundly.

It was the first good night's sleep I'd had since Patti left.

It felt great.

I awoke with new energy.

A new attitude.

A whole new life.

This was going to be great.

I picked up the phone and called my office in New York.

I called my boss. The owner of the company.

He was a total bastard. Would sell his grandmother to make a profit.

Sadly, he thought of me as a son.

Was grooming me to take over one day.

Patti was thrilled about that. I wasn't.

"Where *are* you, Dan?!" he said. "We've got the meeting with Dillard, Smith—"

I cut him off before he went on. There were a *lot* of partners in that firm. And I didn't feel like waiting for him to go through them all.

"I'm not coming in today," I said.

He gasped.

It was the first time he'd ever heard those words come out of *my* mouth.

No matter what, I showed up.

"In fact," I told him. "I'm not coming in ever again!"

His gasp was loud and choked.

"What do you mean?!" he demanded.

"What do I mean?" I repeated. "I mean… I quit!"

"But… but… but…"

"But nothing," I said. "You can take your job and shove it—" But then I stopped. "Never mind. Just know that I quit. I'm never coming back."

"But your office?!" he choked out.

I pictured my office. The diplomas on the walls. The picture of Patti on the desk. The executive toys on the large wooden desk.

It was all worthless to me.

Meaningless.

I couldn't think of one thing that I wanted back.

"Burn it all. I don't care," I said.

I heard him stammering. Fighting to find something to say to me.

I didn't want to hear it.

That too would be meaningless to me.

So I hung up.

I took a deep breath, and shouted with happiness.

I was free!

Elise Leonard

I got dressed. Wore some of Junkyard Dan's old clothes. We were about the same size.

They were all well worn and comfortable.

Nothing fancy. Nothing preppy. Nothing showy. Just practical. And comfortable.

His mother hadn't raised a fool.

Mine had. But *his* hadn't.

This man had his priorities straight.

I fed the dogs and cats. Then went into town to pay for the junkyard.

I met the people in the animal shelter.

They told me wonderful stories of Junkyard Dan. His love for animals. His kind heart.

Then I met with Judge Simpkins. He was a nice man. A short round man with equally round glasses. And a twinkle in his eye.

He was a man who knew more than he let on.

I liked him right away.

We settled the estate in a couple of hours.

He wished me luck. Then he told me that if I ever needed him, to let him know.

He gave me his card.

Then he gave me a few more, "Just in case."

I had no idea what that meant. But he was friendly enough. So I didn't mind.

I popped into the diner. I wanted to tell Hilda that everything was all settled.

I figured I'd leave her a note.

But she was there.

"You're always here!" I said to Hilda. "Do you *sleep* here?!"

I was just kidding.

But she said, "Yes, I have a little room in the back."

I didn't think it was *legal* to sleep in a restaurant in New York.

But as I was finding out? This *wasn't* New York!

Later on, I went back to the junkyard.

I walked around to see the inventory. See what was there.

The man who'd called arrived a few hours after that.

Chapter 17

"Junkyard Dan," he called to me.

I smiled. "That's me."

He walked to me quickly. Then he pumped my hand.

He looked around nervously.

"What's the matter?" I asked him.

"Well, remember those car parts you sold me?" he said quietly.

He looked around again. As if he were checking. Checking to make sure no one was around to hear.

"Not really," I said. "I wasn't here when you bought them."

"Well I bought them here. Take my word," he

said.

He seemed strained. Afraid.

"I want to give them back to you. I don't even want my money back. I just want to give them back to you."

"Why?" I asked.

"They're in my car," he said. "Just take them. I don't want them."

He ran to his car and unlocked his trunk.

He pulled out a few car parts. Old car parts. Used car parts.

How would I even know if he bought them here?!

But he didn't want his money back. So why did I care?!

More inventory for me, I guess.

That's when I noticed. He was wearing rubber gloves.

The big yellow ones.

The kind a woman wears to do dishes. So she doesn't wreck her nails.

Not that Patti ever did the dishes. But we had

the gloves. In case she got an urge.

She never did.

I thought about that.

And it was funny. But when Patti left? She even took the package of rubber gloves.

The thought made me smile.

Neil would find out soon enough.

"What's with the gloves?" I asked.

"I don't want to leave any fingerprints," the man said.

"Why not?" I asked.

Like the old rusty auto parts would care!

I smiled with the thought.

"Because they are encrusted with blood. Lots of blood. Too much blood to be from anything but foul play. Possibly a murder!"

My smile vanished.

"A murder?" I cried out.

He shushed me. And looked around quickly.

"Look. I don't want these. You can do with them what you please. But I don't want them."

"Are all the parts covered with… blood?" I

asked.

"Yes."

"And they all came from the same vehicle?" I asked him.

"Yeah."

"Would you please show me the vehicle?" I asked.

He looked nervous.

"Please," I said. "If what you think is true? I need to find out what happened. I can't do that if I don't know what car the parts came from."

"All right," he whined. "But after I show you? I don't want to be involved."

"Fine," I said. "Just show me the car."

He took me to the far end of the junkyard.

"That's the one," he said.

Then he took off.

I searched the car. And found bloodstains throughout.

The stains could've been mistaken for rust to a pair of old eyes. (Like the old Junkyard Dan's.) But *my* eyes weren't old. And this was definitely blood.

Something had happened in this car.

Something bad. Very bad.

And I felt the need to find out.

First I had to find out who owned this car.

The owner *before* it came to the junkyard.

I looked at a cat that was lying on the roof of the car.

"Well," I said to the cat. "Looks like my quiet, simple life will have to wait a while. At least until I find out what happened in this car."

The cat looked at me and yawned.

Now that you know all the players,

read the next **JUNKYARD DAN** book,

DRIED BLOOD,

to find out what happened to that car!

And whose blood it is!

And if there was a murder in it,

as the customer thought.

Want to read more

JUNKYARD DAN

books?